I0637233

EDWARD'S RHYTHM STICKS

Franklin Willis

Copyright © 2020 by F. Willis Music
All rights reserved. No part of this book may be reproduced
or used in any manner without written permission of the
copyright owner.

ISBN 978-0-578-79164-7

To learn more about Franklin visit his website at:
www.fwillismusic.com

Dedication

This book is dedicated to my son, Edward. Your love of music inspired this book and story. The excitement that comes over your face when you hear music is contagious. My prayer is that you never lose that passion.

You are special. You are brilliant. Your life matters.

Love, Dad.

"Blow out the candles, Edward!" The friends and family who joined together on this special day cheered in celebration of Edward's third birthday.

The time had come for Edward to open his birthday presents, and he was most excited about one gift in particular. Edward knew his grandparents, Glammy and Poppy, always gave him the best gifts.

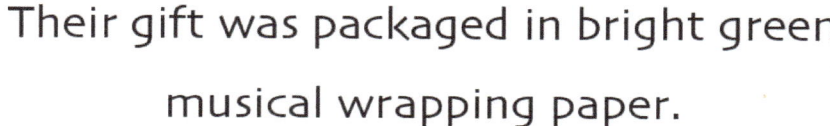

Their gift was packaged in bright green musical wrapping paper.

Edward couldn't wait to see what was in the box. He excitedly tore at the wrapping and pulled out two long sticks the color of blue jays. "Wow, Glammy and Poppy got me rhythm sticks," he exclaimed. "Thank you! Thank you! Thank you!", Edward shouted. "We love you grandson", Poppy replied.

Edward grabbed the sticks and began to dance throughout the house. He clicked them up high, he clicked them down low. He clicked, clicked clicked, wherever he'd go!

The next day Edward brought the rhythm sticks to school. During recess, he took them out and showed his friends the music they made. "Edward, can we play with your rhythm sticks?" asked his friends. "Yes, you can!" he replied. They clicked them up high, they clicked them down low. They clicked, clicked, clicked, wherever they'd go!

Later that evening, Edward clicked, clicked, clicked the rhythm sticks until his mom said, "Edward, put the rhythm sticks down and finish your homework." Edward finished his homework quickly so he could play with his rhythm sticks. He clicked them up high, he clicked them down low. He clicked, clicked, clicked, wherever he'd go!

At the dinner table, Edward clicked, clicked, clicked the rhythm sticks until his Dad said, "Son, put the rhythm sticks down and eat your food."

Edward replied, "Yes, sir...but, can I play them one more time? Please Dad?" Edward's Dad said, "Yes, but you can only play them one more time and it must be very soft."

Edward replied, "Yes sir, you are the best dad!" So, very softly, he clicked them up high, he clicked them down low. He clicked, clicked, clicked, wherever he'd go!

Early Sunday morning, Edward dressed for church.
He put on his blue suit to match his blue rhythm sticks.
Edward couldn't wait to hear the church musicians and
the soulful voices of the choir. As they played, he clicked,
clicked, clicked the rhythm sticks. He clicked them up
high, he clicked them down low. He clicked, clicked,
clicked wherever he'd go!

After church, Edward and his Dad went to the barbershop to get haircuts. As Edward waited for his haircut, he clicked, clicked, clicked the rhythm sticks. He clicked them up high, he clicked them down low. He clicked, clicked, clicked, wherever he'd go! Cousin V, his barber, called out to Edward, "Hey, you're up next, but you can't play your rhythm sticks while you are getting your haircut." Edward placed his rhythm sticks on a nearby table filled with magazines and ran to the barber chair.

While getting his haircut, Edward fell asleep.

His Dad gently picked him up and carried him to the car.

Edward slept the whole way home.

Later that afternoon Edward woke up looking for his rhythm sticks. He looked up high, he looked down low and wondered to himself, "Where oh where did my rhythm sticks go?" Edward cried out to his parents, "I can't find my rhythm sticks!" His parents helped him look for his rhythm sticks everywhere around the house. They looked up high, they looked down low, but they could not find the two long sticks the color of blue jays.

Edward's mom finally said, "I'm sorry we can't find your rhythm sticks Edward. Let's go in the backyard and get some fresh air." As they sat on the backyard steps, Edward noticed a tree limb. On that limb, he saw two small branches that reminded him of his blue rhythm sticks. He jumped up, tore the two branches away and... he clicked them up high, he clicked them down low. He clicked, clicked, clicked, wherever he'd go!

Edward's mom watched him dance with the two branches around the backyard. Puzzled, she asked, "What are you doing Edward?" "I am making music with my new rhythm sticks! Music is everywhere!", he replied. Edward's Mom smiled in agreement and said, "that's right Edward, music is everywhere!" Edward continued to dance with the branches, he clicked them up high, he clicked them down low. He clicked, clicked, clicked, wherever he'd go!

After playing with his new rhythm sticks, Edward and his mom made their way back into the house. As they walked in, they heard a familiar voice talking to dad at the door. Edward took a closer look and saw Cousin V the barber holding his blue rhythm sticks.

Edward jumped for JOY! He thanked Cousin V
and started jamming with his blue rhythm sticks.
He clicked them up high, he clicked them down low.
He clicked, clicked, clicked, wherever he'd go!

Music is Everywhere!

Edward's Rhythm Sticks is a story that shows how much music is a part of our lives. This story illustrates the joy of music making and how even the simplest things can be made into instruments. This story is a great way for children to learn rhythm, pattern and sequence. Most of all, parents and teachers can use this engaging book to connect learning, music, literacy and having fun together. Join Edward on this rhythmic journey as he shares his love of music with his friends, family, and community.

About the Author:

Franklin Willis is a music educator, entrepreneur, husband and dad. Franklin's educational philosophy stems around the belief that every child has musical potential. He specializes in providing musical instruction through authentic culturally relevant teaching experiences to engage all children to achieve personal success. This book was written to empower students to embrace music in different forms.

To learn more about Franklin visit his website at: www.fwillismusic.com

101120-100-1-80#Gloss

www.ingramcontent.com/pod-product-compliance
Lightning Source LLC
Chambersburg PA
CBHW041541240626
47164CB00002B/84

* 9 7 8 0 5 7 8 7 9 1 6 4 7 *